reboot your brain

Reboot Your Brain

Tim Shoemaker

illustrated by Marty Baumann

smarter • stronger
2:52
deeper • cooler

Zonder**kidz**

Zonder**kidz**®

The children's group of Zondervan

www.zonderkidz.com

Reboot Your Brain
Copyright © 2004 by Tim Shoemaker
Illustrations © 2004 by Marty Baumann

Requests for information should be addressed to:
Grand Rapids, Michigan 49530

ISBN: 0-310-70719-6

Editor: Amy De Vries
Interior design: Tobias Design
Art direction: Michelle Lenger

Printed in the United States

04 05 06 07 /❖ RRD/ 5 4 3 2 1

DEDICATED TO

Gabe and Brandan.
In a world of choices, may you make the right ones.

And to Madelyn and Megan.
This may have been written for boys,
but there's a whole lot here for you too.

ACKNOWLEDGMENTS

Special thanks to Andy, Mark, and Luke Shoemaker along with Kevin, Karl, and Kristy Sorensen for their ideas that helped make this book even more fun.

CONTENTS

A Word from the Author 8

Introduction 9

They Don't Go *Looking* for Trouble,
but Somehow It Seems to Find Them 10
> Meet the regulars of the "Code 2:52"
> comic series.

1. Big Mouth ... Big Trouble 16
> Frustrated that he can't beat a pinball
> game, Troy makes some comments that
> almost get him a real beating!

2. Pride Ride 28
> The opportunity to show off a little seems
> harmless to Troy until things start falling
> apart!

3. High Tide 40
> Instead of "forgive and forget," Howie
> masterminds a "get even" prank that
> leaves Troy in deep water.

4. Operation Obnoxious 53
> Troy thinks an annoying girl at school is a
> big problem ... wait till he takes
> Eddie's advice about how to deal with her!

5. It Pays To Be Selfish? 68
> Eddie's habit of "looking out for #1"

6. Eddie and the Homemade Stink Bombs   82

Eddie's idea of patience is taking the time to pull off the perfect prank.

7. The Homework Assignment   94

David is forced to make a quick choice between honesty and "covering" for Eddie.

8. Anger Essay   106

Troy learns a little about anger . . . the hard way!

9. Eddie and the Green-Eyed Monster   119

Things go from bad to worse when Eddie lets jealousy get the best of him.

10. The Palm Reader   134

Troy wishes he'd done the right thing after a wrong choice leads to a real nightmare.

A Note to the Reader   149

A WORD FROM THE AUTHOR

Computers are great, but they aren't perfect. Sometimes they run into a "glitch." When that happens to my computer, I reboot. The computer restarts and usually runs fine because it got rid of the bad stuff.

You and I can be a little like a computer. There are times when we're not operating or living the way God designed us to live. Sometimes we don't even notice that a glitch has developed in our life.

This book will help you get rid of the bad stuff—"reboot" your brain. It will remind you that God designed you to live so you can grow in wisdom and in favor with God and man.

Each chapter includes a new episode of "Code 2:52"—a comic about four guys who often make wrong choices and get themselves into *real* messes—and a great Bible story to guide you in knowing what is right. These comics and the stories from God's Word can help you get a better handle on how God wants you to live.

When your life runs into a glitch, just "reboot" your brain!

—Tim Shoemaker

AND JESUS GREW IN WISDOM AND STATURE, AND IN FAVOR WITH GOD AND MEN. —LUKE 2:52

This verse tells us that as Jesus grew bigger, he was getting smarter too. God and people loved him. Doesn't it make you wonder *what* Jesus did that made others like him so much? It wasn't just that he was so wise and smart. He was wise about how he lived and treated people.

LET LOVE AND FAITHFULNESS NEVER LEAVE YOU; BIND THEM AROUND YOUR NECK, WRITE THEM ON THE TABLET OF YOUR HEART. THEN YOU WILL WIN FAVOR AND A GOOD NAME IN THE SIGHT OF GOD AND MAN. —PROVERBS 3:3-4

There they are ... those same words about "favor" with "God and man." Love and faithfulness are the keys. Jesus was *faithful* to God and others. Jesus *loved* God and others. That means Jesus lived according to the love described in 1 Corinthians 13. Love is patient. Love is kind and honest. Love does not envy. It doesn't boast. And it's not proud. Love isn't easily angered. It's not selfish or rude. Love doesn't get a kick out of evil. Love forgives.

Jesus put all of these principles into practice. People couldn't help but love him. He really *was* smart, wasn't he?

We can be smarter too by showing more love to others. In this book we'll take a look at some ways we can do that. When you put these principles into practice, you'll find that most people will appreciate you more, even brothers and sisters! Hey, you don't always need a teacher to help you get smarter. Since you've read this far, you're *already* getting smarter.

THEY DON'T GO LOOKING FOR TROUBLE, BUT SOMEHOW IT SEEMS TO FIND THEM

Meet the regulars of the "Code 2:52" comic series.

David Callahan

- Responsible and even tempered, the unofficial leader of the group.

- Quiet (when compared to the others), cares for others.

- Thirteen years old, in eighth grade at Hudson J. Ford Junior High, has two younger sisters.

- Rededicated his life to Christ in seventh grade while on a church youth group retreat. The youth pastor's challenge to be more like Christ, as described in Luke 2:52, impacted him deeply.

- Encourages Troy and Howie to be more like Jesus with something he calls "Code 2:52," referring to the principles he learned in Luke 2:52.

- Has been reaching out to Eddie and his sister, Mallory, and hopes they will become Christians.

Troy McBride, "Trigger"

- Very competitive and hates to lose.

- Loves almost all sports, but basketball is his passion.

- Strong-willed and tends to act and speak before he thinks.

- Thirteen years old, in eighth grade, has two brothers, one older, one younger.

- Rededicated his life to Christ when David did.

- Got the nickname "Trigger" because of his quick temper, although he has gotten much better at controlling it. Most kids who didn't know him before junior high think his nickname came from his ability to sink 'em in basketball.

zachary Howard piccolino, "Howie"

- Hyperactive and slightly unpredictable.

- Will try anything. Loves demolition-type work, like gutting an apartment with his dad.

- Independent, doesn't seem to care what people think of him.

- Weird is normal for him. He likes to wear crazy T-shirts he buys at thrift stores. Has broken more bones than the rest of the group collectively.

- Comes off as a clown, but doesn't try to be funny. That's just the way he is.

- Loves pulling off a good prank.

- Thirteen years old, in eighth grade, has two older sisters who don't understand him at all.

- Struggles in school.

- Growing as a Christian, but not as serious about his faith as David and Troy.

- Nicknamed "Howie" by his older sister Shirley, and the name stuck.

eddie Thatcher

- Funny, "life of the party," but often doesn't have the sense to know when to stop.

- Doesn't consider himself to be lazy, but is skilled at avoiding work.

- He could be athletic, but doesn't make an effort to sharpen his skills.

- Thirteen years old, in eighth grade, lives with his mom, older brother, and younger sister, Mallory.

- Doesn't see his dad as much as he'd like since the divorce, but acts like it doesn't bother him.

- His mom and brother work a lot, so he is forced to let Mallory tag along, which he usually doesn't mind.

- Not a Christian.

- Considers David, Troy, and Howie his best friends.
  The fact is, they are his only friends.

Mallory Thatcher, the "Kid"

- Doesn't feel comfortable with other girls her age.

- Prefers hanging out with her brother, Eddie, and the other guys, and isn't intimidated by them.

- Not afraid to speak her mind.

- Fiercely loyal to Eddie and the other guys in the group, but rarely shows it.

- Ten years old, but has grown up faster than most girls her age.

- Not a Christian, but her respect for David has made her more open to it.

- The guys refer to her as the "Kid," and she doesn't mind a bit.

Two others stay very close to the group,

but nobody has ever seen them.

gabe

(not *the* gabriel we read about in the bible)

- An angel of the Lord assigned to be an extra guardian over David, Howie, and Troy.

- Quiet, yet very powerful. Has a sword strapped in a sheath at his side.

- He *can't* be seen by any human, but can speak to a person's conscience.

slick

- A demon from Satan's legions of darkness.

- Has direct orders to discourage and destroy David, Troy, and Howie in any way he can.

- Has further orders to keep Eddie and Mallory from becoming true believers in Jesus.

- Comes across as a wise-cracking prankster. That is just a cover. Inside he is seething with a demonic lust to destroy Christians and see Eddie and Mallory ushered into hell.

- He *can't* be seen by any human, but he can plant thoughts in a person's head.

CHAPTER 1

"Big Mouth...Big Trouble"
email from Troy

To: Every guy who has ever said something he *shouldn't* have said
Subject: Me and my *BIG* mouth

****

I *know* I'm not the only guy out there with a mouth problem. Tell me you hear things like, "Watch your mouth!" "Don't talk fresh!" "Don't talk like that to your mother!" (Or sister, or brother) "Don't give me any of your lip!"

It's not that I *can't* say things in a nice way, it's just that often I don't. My mouth gets ahead of my brain. And it gets me in *big* trouble.

This happens to you, too . . . right? Why do we *do* that? But I've learned my lesson. I came close to having my face rearranged by a kid who didn't like what I said.

I'm asking God to help me watch my mouth . . . before somebody gets another chance to knock my teeth out.

Trying to zip my lip,

Troy

****

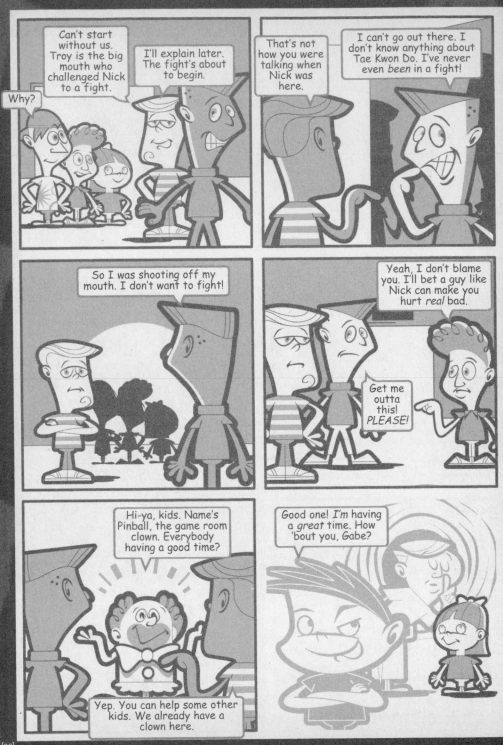

How the Man with the Biggest Mouth in the World Lost His Head

You gotta eat a lot of pancakes to grow to over nine feet tall! We're not sure what Goliath's mom fed him, but he must have cleaned his plate. At every meal.

Goliath was a soldier in the Philistine army, and had a mouth to match his overgrown size. His army chose Goliath to be the spokesman to challenge the Israelite army to fight. Day after day Goliath shouted over to the Israelites' campsite. He dared any Israelite to fight him. He taunted, he teased. He insulted the Israelite soldiers, and by doing that, he was insulting God too. Yeah, he had a big mouth, but when he insulted God he proved he didn't have a giant-sized brain.

See, Goliath overlooked one thing. God hears what people say, and he *cares* about what people say. Now God was going to teach Goliath a lesson.

Young David the shepherd came to visit his brothers, who were soldiers in the Israelite army. David heard Goliath mocking the terrified Israelite soldiers.

David offered to fight Goliath, and God used him to "cut" Goliath down to size.

Yeah, David pegged the big guy in the head with a stone slung with his slingshot. To the shock of the armies, the human skyscraper thundered to the ground.

David wasn't surprised. He knew God didn't appreciate Goliath's big mouth. God made our mouths to eat with, encourage others, and help others. Goliath had the eating part figured out just fine, but he didn't have a clue about the other stuff.

David ran over to where the giant was sprawled out on the ground like a rolled-over semi. He slid Goliath's sword out of its sheath and whacked Goliath's head clean off. Thwack! Then David actually picked up Goliath's head and took it to town. Yeah, he brought the big guy's head to Jerusalem so everyone could see it. Like some kind of trophy. Whoa. I've seen all kinds of trophies. But a human head?

I guess God was making the point big time about watching our mouths. A big mouth can get us in big trouble.

I'm not saying that if you shoot your mouth off God will send someone to your house carrying a sling. God hears everything you say. If you use your mouth in the wrong way, he won't be pleased. We need to be careful about what we say. Hey, if you want friends, family, and especially God to appreciate you more, watch your mouth!

Want to read the story of David and Goliath in the Bible? You'll find it in 1 Samuel, chapter 17.

HOW BRAINY ARE YOU?

OK, if I want my family and friends to enjoy and appreciate me more, I've figured out I have to watch my mouth. But I have to ask God for help on that 'cause I'm not doing so good on my own. It's the little things that get me in trouble.

How about you? How are you doing when it comes to watching what you say? Take this little quiz and you'll find out. Pick the answer that best describes you.

Howie

1.   When your mom or dad tells you to do something that you aren't exactly excited about doing, you should:
   A.   Tell them you'll do it later when you get a chance.
   B.   Complain about it to see if they'll change their mind.
   C.   Argue with them about doing it, especially if you think the job should really be done by your brother or sister.
   D.   Have a good attitude and obey pronto.

2.   When your brother or sister is bothering you by the way they are acting or talking, you should:
   A.   Give 'em a piece of your mind.
   B.   Shut 'em up with a real zinger of an insult.
   C.   Haul off and whack 'em if Mom or Dad isn't looking.
   D.   Watch your mouth so you don't sin.

3.   If someone calls you a mean name you should:
   A.   Call them the same name right back.
   B.   Say, "I know you are, but what am I?"

C. Say something even more insulting back to them.

D. Say something nice back to them or don't say anything at all.

4. **If you have the perfect opportunity to say something that will make someone look or feel like a fool, you should:**

A. Say it real loud so other people will know how funny you are.

B. Say it. You don't get a perfect opportunity every day.

C. Say it. People do it to you all the time.

D. Keep your mouth shut.

5. **If you see someone who is being teased or insulted and is obviously hurt and discouraged, you should:**

A. Join in the teasing and make him feel even more like an idiot.

B. Walk away and pretend you never heard or saw it.

C. Shrug it off. They probably deserve it. Besides, it's none of your business.

D. In a nice way try to get the person to stop teasing and say something nice to the person who was being teased.

How did you do? If you chose answer "D" for each one, I gotta say "congratulations." You're on your way. Keep it up!

FAQS

(FREQUENTLY ASKED QUESTIONS)

These are questions guys ask. I didn't come up with the answers on my own. I got some good help. Check these out.—David

1. **Is it OK to say something nasty to your sister if she really deserves it?**
   I wish that were OK. Unfortunately we can't talk nasty to a sister, brother or anyone else no matter how much that person deserves it. If I talk in a mean way to my sister, that's sin. If I sin, I'm in as much trouble in God's eyes as my sister probably is. God wants us to treat others with patience and kindness, no matter how they treat us. Check out 1 Corinthians 13:4–7.

2. **What am I supposed to do when someone is talking rudely to me?**
   Be respectful and hang in there. Don't resort to being rude. If you do, you'll only make things worse. Remember Proverbs 15:1: "A gentle answer turns away wrath, but a harsh word stirs up anger."

3. **If I say something kind of mean about someone, but they don't hear me, is that OK?**
   Sorry. That still isn't a good thing. In fact, it's wrong. Read 1 Corinthians 13:4–7 again. Notice that it doesn't say anything about showing

love to a person only when that person is around.

4. **Sometimes I say kind of mean things that later I regret (sort of). Can you help me out?**

    I don't think there's a person on earth who doesn't struggle with this. You need to tell the person you hurt that you're sorry and admit that what you said was wrong. Memorize Psalm 141:3. That verse asks God to "set a guard over my mouth." Rather than trying to control your mouth on your own, ask God to help.

5. **Some of my friends from school swear a lot. Sometimes I do too, even though I know it's wrong. How can I stop?**

    This could be tough, especially if swearing has become a habit. Look at Psalm 141:3–4. It says: "Set a guard over my mouth, O Lord; keep watch over the door of my lips. Let not my heart be drawn to what is evil, to take part in wicked deeds with men who are evildoers."

    This is a good prayer to help you. You're asking God to help you watch your mouth and to keep you from getting sucked in by the crowd to do things that aren't right. It can be tough to stop swearing, but with God's help, you can do it.

    One last thought. If your friends are a bad influence on you, you need to look for new ones. First Corinthians 15:33 warns us that "bad company corrupts good character." It's better to lose friends than to be corrupted by the ones you have.

CHAPTER 2

"pride ride"
email from troy

To: Every guy who has let his pride get him in trouble
Subject: Remind me not to go back to the mall ... ever!

****

I want you to get this straight from me, not from what others are saying. I was only trying to show off. I didn't think anything bad could happen. I mean, hey, Eddie's kid sister was acting like she thought I was a wimp. I had to do something. What would *you* have done?

It was just a freak accident. Eddie loved every horrifying second of it. I was still shaking when I got home.

At first I blamed Eddie. It was his idea. The truth is, I can't blame anyone but myself. I didn't have to do it. But I wanted to prove how strong I was. It was a pride thing. And that was stupid.

The next time I feel the need to prove how strong I am, I'll stick with something safe—like push-ups. Better yet, maybe I'll try something that takes even *more* strength—being humble.

Learning that pride is right there before a fall,

Troy

****

the strong man's weakness

He fought thirty different men in a single night. He killed them all. Later, while seeking revenge for the murder of his wife, he single-handedly slaughtered many of the men involved in her death. When the Philistine army was sent to take him prisoner, he easily snapped the ropes they used to tie his arms together. He had no weapon, so he grabbed the jawbone from a nearby donkey skeleton. He swung that jawbone like a battle axe and killed a thousand men from the enemy army. Yeah, Samson was strong.

But Samson was undone by one dangerous weakness—pride. He was proud of how strong he was. One night the Philistines trapped him in a walled city. They locked the gates, figuring they'd go in and get him in the morning. In the middle of the night he got up and ripped the gates and the posts right out of the wall. He carried them to a nearby hill just to show off a little that he had escaped. He was so used to being able to get out of any trouble that he stopped being careful. He even got careless about obeying God. That wasn't smart, because God was the one who gave Samson his superhuman strength.

Samson fell in love with a bad woman. Her name was Delilah. The Philistines paid her to find the secret of his great strength. Three times she helped the Philistines lay traps for Samson, but every time he escaped. Samson, in his pride, figured he could escape *any* trap. Delilah laid a fourth trap, and this time God didn't bail

Samson out. The Philistines captured him and gouged out his eyes so he could never escape again.

Pride has a way of blinding all of us. We see ourselves as bigger, stronger, or more important than others. We put ourselves first. All we see is what *we* want.

Samson began to see things a lot more clearly *after* he was blind. He became humble and asked God to use him again to destroy the Philistines, the terrible enemies of his people. God answered his prayer. For one last time, God gave Samson superhuman strength so he could push down the pillars and collapse a huge Philistine temple loaded with his enemies. Thousands of Philistines died as the temple came crashing down on them. In fact he destroyed more enemy Philistines in that one display of strength than he had in all the rest of his entire life. I guess it proves one thing—a humble person is the strongest of all.

Want to read the story of Samson straight from the Bible? Read Judges chapters 13—16.

HOW BRAINY ARE YOU?

Our little escapade on the escalator at the mall taught me a lot about pride. Let's see how well you do on this quiz.

Howie

1. **Which one of these gives the best example of pride?**
   A. Picking up a penny you find on the ground.
   B. Taking out the garbage.
   C. Showing off your expensive new basketball.

2. **It's OK to brag about how good you are as long as it's true.**
   A. Sure, it reminds other kids you're better than they are.
   B. No, bragging is a form of pride.

3. **If you have a "me first" attitude or believe you're better than others,**
   A. There's nothing wrong with that.
   B. It's OK. You're probably just a natural leader.
   C. It doesn't mean you have a pride problem.
   D. It *does* mean you have a pride problem.

4. **When can pride take place in your heart?**
   A. At school.
   B. At home.
   C. When you look in a mirror.
   D. All of the above.

How did you do? The last answer of each is the right answer.

FAQS
(FREQUENTLY
ASKED QUESTIONS)

God hates pride, so it makes sense that we look at it a little bit so we can stay away from it. Here are some questions I asked a man at church, along with his answers. They really helped me.—David

1. **I worked hard and did a good job on a project for school. I was told, "You should be proud of yourself." Is it wrong to be proud of myself?**
    Think about it this way. A man builds a computer. He plugs it in to give it power. He loads it with memory and programs that allow it to do almost anything. If the computer could think, would it be right for it to be "proud" of something it did? Hardly.

    It's the same with us. God gives us a brain, abilities, and life itself. We wouldn't even exist without him. When people compliment us on something we did, we have to be careful not to start feeling so proud inside that we think we deserve all the credit. We need to remember to give the credit to God. That's where it belongs. Without God, you could do nothing.

2. **My teacher wrote a note on the side of my paper that said, "Take a little more pride in your work." You're telling me I need less pride, but my teacher says I need more. What's the story?**

    What your teacher is saying is that you need to do a better job, put more effort into your work. She believes you're capable of doing better, but you don't because you're too lazy to work up to your potential. When you work below your abilities, it gives you a bad reputation. Your teacher is telling you to care enough about your reputation to do a better job. Read Proverbs 22:1 to see how valuable it is to have a "good name," or reputation. Remember, too, that if you're a Christian, what you do affects God's reputation.

3. **What's wrong with bragging a little?**

    Bragging leaves God out. Bragging is saying, "Hey, look at me. Look what I did." Bragging doesn't figure in that you couldn't have done a single thing without God. Who gave you life, abilities, health, and a good mind? If you want to brag, the one you should brag about is God. Check out what you can boast about in 1 Corinthians 1:31 and Galatians 6:14. One more thought. The opposite of someone who brags is someone who is humble. Check out what God says in James 4:6 about how he reacts to guys who are proud and those who are humble.

4. **A little pride doesn't seem like such a big deal. It's not like I'm murdering someone. Why does God hate it so much?**

    Pride is a big deal. It was pride that got in Satan's heart and made him rebel against God. Pride was the beginning, and all the other sins and misery followed. Pride is taking credit yourself when the credit really belongs to God. That's stealing. Pride is dangerous. People underestimate its power to hurt them. The devil loves to trap people with it. Pride has destroyed many, many people.

God loves you and hates pride. He doesn't want you to get suckered into being proud, which will hurt you and damage your relationship with him. Pride is first on God's short list of things he hates most. Check out Proverbs 6:16–17. "Haughty eyes" means pride. See Proverbs 16:18 if you have any doubts about the extreme danger of pride.

CHAPTER 3

"High Tide"
email from Troy

To: Any guy who has ever had a hard time forgiving someone
Subject: The high price of revenge

****

I wish I had listened to David. He told all of us to "forgive and forget." He warned us that the prank was a bad idea. I thought he was just being a wimp.

I wanted to teach some guy a lesson. He had been mean to the kid. I wanted revenge. Haven't you felt that way too?

If I had taken David's advice, I'd be out shooting hoops instead of sitting in my room, grounded. I keep replaying the whole thing in my mind. Especially the end. I *know* I moved that hose out of the way. I'll never figure out how I tripped over it. And got caught.

Anyway, the next time I feel the need to get even, I plan to be smart and get over it instead. Forgive and forget about it. Maybe someday I'll even forgive Eddie for getting me into that mess!

Sincerely sorry,

Troy

****

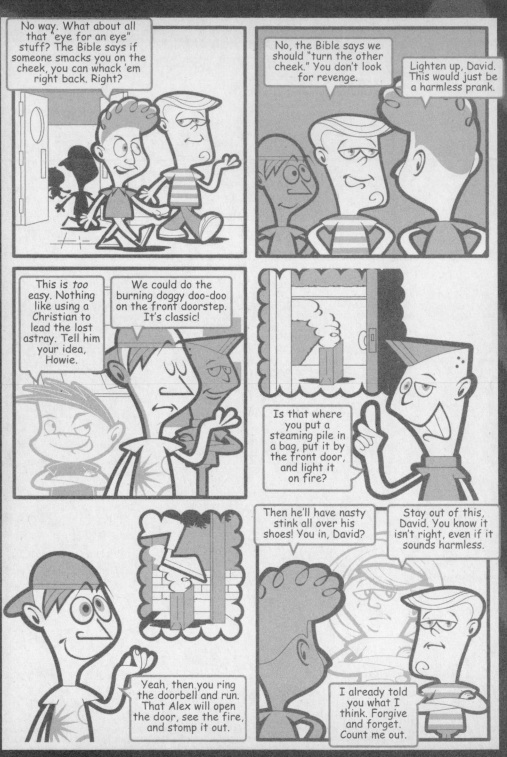

Beyond stupid

Jesus told a story of a guy he referred to as a "wicked servant." Some might have called him a "stupid servant" or maybe a "foolish servant." This servant owed so much money to his king that it would have been impossible for him to pay it all back. The king, to help make up for at least part of his loss, ordered that the servant, his wife, and his kids be sold as slaves.

The servant fell on his knees and begged for mercy, just like you or I would have done. The king felt sorry for him and decided to forgive the debt his servant owed and set him free. The servant didn't have to pay the king anything.

Then the servant did something really stupid. The servant found a man who owed *him* a little money and demanded that the man pay him, *pronto*. The man begged for mercy, but, like a real jerk, the king's servant had the man thrown in jail!

When the king heard about what his servant had done, he was really ticked off. He had his servant come before him for a little "talk." The king told the man something like, "I forgave you for all the money you owed me, and I had mercy on you. You should have done the same thing for the guy who owed *you* money." The king was so angry that he had his servant thrown in jail to be held as a prisoner and tortured until he could pay back all the money he owed the king.

In telling this story, Jesus was trying to get a message across about how we need to have mercy on others and to forgive them. Jesus forgave our mountain of sin and made it clear that we need to forgive others. If we don't, we're just as stupid as the king's servant. Jesus called him "wicked." You know what? I think he *did* pick the best word. When we don't forgive others, we're beyond stupid. We're wicked.

Want to read it in the Bible for yourself? Read Matthew 18:21–35.

HOW BRAINY ARE YOU?

Let's see how much you know about forgiveness. I put this little quiz together a couple of days after our little "High Tide" prank bombed.

Howie

1. **Your friend says something mean about you and later tells you he's sorry. You forgive him, and he does the same thing to you again. What should you do?**
   A. Don't forgive him the second time.
   B. Hit him.
   C. When he apologizes, tell him you'll think about it. Make him sweat for a while.
   D. Forgive him again.

2. **When you really forgive someone,**
   A. You can still hold a grudge against them as long as they don't know it.
   B. You still have the right to hurt them back if you get the chance.
   C. It's OK to hate them forever.
   D. You have to get over it. You can't keep resenting the person.

3. When you forgive someone, you need to stop resenting what they did for how long?

    A. One month

    B. One year

    C. Five years

    D. Forever

4. Can a person do something so bad that you really don't have to forgive them, even if they ask you to?

    A. Absolutely. Some things are just unforgivable.

    B. No. Since God forgives us, we have to forgive others, no matter what they do. (Of course, God gave us a brain, too. Forgiving doesn't mean we keep letting a person hurt us. Sometimes we need to make new friends or get help to protect us from an abusive situation. Forgiving someone else doesn't mean we simply allow ourselves to be put in a position to be hurt again.)

How did you do?
The right answer is always the last one.

FAQS

(FREQUENTLY ASKED QUESTIONS)

Forgiveness is something I don't think about. Normally. When I was a little kid, my mom would have to remind me to say "I'm sorry" when I did something bad. And I always felt better when she'd say, "You're forgiven." Now I'm beginning to find out just how important it is to forgive. Here are some questions from guys like you that I gave to a leader at our church to try to get some answers. There's some good stuff in here.—David

1. **How many times am I supposed to forgive someone who does something wrong to me?**

   Peter asked Jesus the same question in Matthew 18:21–22. He made it pretty clear that you need to keep forgiving a person who wrongs you. Look at it this way. God keeps forgiving you, right? In the same way, we're to forgive others. Now, if you have a "friend" who keeps hurting you in some way, you probably should look for a new friend. Just because we need to forgive others doesn't mean we have to put ourselves in a position to keep getting hurt.

2. **Should I forgive someone even if they haven't told me that they're sorry for what they did?**

   Yes. If we don't forgive someone, deep inside we may hold a grudge against them. That can turn to bitterness. Bitterness is like a poison that can destroy us in many ways. The point is, we're only hurting ourselves if we don't forgive the person and let it go. Check out the example of Joseph in Genesis 45. It's pretty obvious he had forgiven his brothers long before he saw them again. He had forgiven them and moved on. He was a better man for it.

3. **How can I possibly forgive someone who hurt me really bad?**

   This is tough. You need to ask God to help you, but you have to forgive for your own good. If you don't, you'll mess yourself up worse. Think about it. God is willing to forgive every person on Earth for every single sin they've committed. Who are you to say that you won't forgive someone that God is willing to forgive? You're putting yourself in authority over God, and that's crazy. In Matthew 6:14–15 Jesus makes it clear that you need to forgive others. "But if you do not forgive men their sins, your Father will not forgive your sins." That's serious stuff.

   For those times when you find it really tough to forgive, ask God for his help. Remember Philippians 4:13, "I can do everything through him who gives me strength."

   Remember, forgiving is the right thing to do, but that doesn't mean you just let a person hurt you again. If you've been abused physically or emotionally, you need to get help. If you have "friends" who are mean, maybe you need to find new ones.

4. **I keep hearing people tell me to "forgive and forget." I get the forgiving part, but does God really expect me to forget?**

You may never totally forget what was done to you, but you forget about it in the sense that you don't let it bother you anymore. You definitely don't bring it up again and again and use it against the person who wronged you. First Corinthians 13:5 tells us that love doesn't keep a "record of wrongs." When you truly forgive someone from the heart as Jesus tells us to do in Matthew 18:35, you let go of your right to hold a grudge against that person. Ask God to help you with this. It's amazing how he can help you forgive and forget.

"operation obnoxious"
email from Troy

To: Every one of you who has ever been given bad advice—and taken it
Subject: I wish I hadn't listened to Eddie

****

I know, I know. What was I thinking? Eddie gave me advice. David gave me advice. I went with Eddie. Stupid, stupid, stupid. Taking advice from Eddie is like ripping the railing off the balcony of a fourth-story apartment. Or riding a bike with a blindfold on. It's *dangerous!*

I cringe when I think about the mean things I said. You know the feeling. You say or do something mean to someone and then feel rotten.

I'm keeping a roll of duct tape in my backpack now. The next time I'm tempted to say something nasty, I'm going to whip out that roll and slap a piece of tape over my mouth. I don't want to feel this miserable again.

Praying for a "kind" mind,

Troy

****

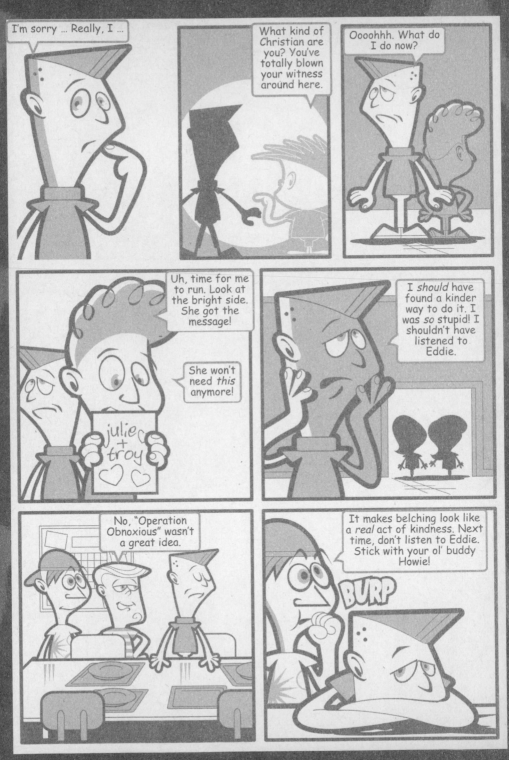

Lucky Loser

diot. Loser. Moron. Geek. Lots of names are used to refer to kids who don't seem to fit in.

We've all seen it happen. Some unlucky kid becomes a target for other kids to nail with cruel insults and teasing. When someone is labeled, there isn't much that person can do to change it, although many try. Even when they try to break out and be funny or cool or smart, it usually backfires.

In the Bible, there's a story about a man who didn't fit in. He wasn't just a guy who got labeled a "loser." He was possessed by a clan of demons. They made this poor guy act truly *weird*. Freaky. The demons made him incredibly strong and made him do bizarre things, like use sharp rocks to cut himself. He didn't have *any* friends. Zero. Zip.

More than once the people from town tried to chain him up. The man always busted free. He made the Hulk look like a wimp.

The man was miserable. He lived in the graveyard, where he could get away from people, at least the ones still alive.

When Jesus visited the area, the man fell on his knees in front of him. Jesus wasn't mean to him like everyone else was. He reached out to help the man and got rid of the demons. In an instant, the man was normal. Because of Jesus, he wasn't a loser anymore. In fact, most people would consider the man to be downright *lucky*.

Jesus sent the man back to town to tell people what Jesus had done for him. The people who had once looked at the man as a loser were amazed! Jesus changed that tormented man into a trophy of God's love.

That transformation started with kindness. Jesus was kind to a man other people didn't like. He cared about someone that nobody else cared about. Did you ever think that Jesus might want *you* to do the same? Yeah, he may want *you* to reach out in kindness to kids who aren't treated nicely by others. As Christians, we're supposed to act like Jesus. That means we need to be kind to *all* kinds of people. God may want to use us to help save another person from a life of misery.

Can you think of someone who has been labeled a loser? Be like Jesus and be kind to that person. With your kindness, you can make a real difference in their life by showing them how much Jesus loves them. God can use your kindness to transform a kid who has been labeled a loser and make him feel like the luckiest kid around!

Want to read it straight from the Bible? Read Mark 5:1–20.

HOW BRAINY ARE YOU?

I was sitting right there at the table when Trigger said those nasty things about "the moose." I hate to admit it, but when I saw her crying, I felt bad for her. It made me wonder how often I hurt people by the things I do or say. I decided I need to be more kind.

Check out this quiz. I had some trouble with question 4. Answers "B" and "C" looked pretty good to me. See what you think.

Howie

1. **Which one of these is an example of kindness?**
    A. Punching someone.
    B. Taking a person's lunch money.
    C. Making fun of someone.
    D. Helping a friend do their chores.

2. **Showing kindness to others is always easy to do.**
    A. True
    B. False

3. **You're walking down the hallway at school and see a bully shove a kid into the lockers and knock his books and papers to the floor. What should you do?**

A. Walk by and pretend you didn't see what happened.

B. Kick the papers and books a little as you go by, as if you didn't see them.

C. Punch the bully (who happens to be twice your size).

D. Help the kid pick up his books and papers.

4. **Fill in the blank with the best choice.**
   There is always time to _____.

A. Be rude.

B. Watch TV.

C. Raid the refrigerator.

D. Be kind.

How did you do? The right answer is the last choice for each question.

FAQS

(FREQUENTLY

ASKED QUESTIONS)

Has anyone ever done something really kind for you? I remember when a guy at school did something kind for me. I hardly even knew him. It had a real impact on me. I want to help others the way he helped me. It's one way that I, as a Christian, can make a difference. Here are some questions I gave to a leader at our church. I hope his answers help you as much as they helped me.—David

1. **I pretty much ignore girls. It's not that I'm trying to be rude, it's just that if I'm nice to them, they might think I like them. That's OK, isn't it?**

   We need to be nice, even to girls. Let's face it, at this age girls can be ...well ... difficult. Some will think you like them even if you're mean to them. The thing is, the Bible tells us to treat others in a nice way, and that includes girls. I'm not saying you have to get chummy with everyone. Just be nice and polite.

2. **How can I be kind to someone who is a real idiot?**

   Tough question. You need to ask God to help you to be kind. Don't try to do it on your own. Look at Jesus' example. He was ultimately kind to a

world of sinners when he gave his life for us all on the cross.
Read Romans 5:6—8.

3. There's a kid at school who is always getting teased. If I
start being nice to him, won't other kids think I'm weird?

They might. They might start teasing you, too. Remember,
Jesus reached out to the "losers" of this world, and he wants
you to do the same. These kids need someone to walk with and
encourage them. Maybe that's one reason why God has you in
the same class with that kid. He wants to make a difference in
his life through you. And you know what? You'll be glad you did.
I can still remember some losers in school that I didn't reach
out to and I really, really regret it. Don't make that mistake.
Ask Jesus to help you to be more like him.

If other kids give you a hard time about being kind to losers,
study 1 Peter 2:20—25, which tells us not to retaliate or threat-
en to get even when someone is mean to us.

4. Why should I bother to be kind to someone who isn't kind
to me?

We're supposed to grow to be more like Jesus, right? Well,
Jesus was kind to all types of people, even those who weren't
kind to him. Check out Matthew 5:43—48 and 1 Peter 2:21—25.
Don't try to be kind to everyone on your own, though. Ask God
for help. The Holy Spirit will give you the power to do it.

CHAPTER 5

"It pays to be selfish?"
email from Troy

To: Every guy who has ever done something selfish (that's all of us)
Subject: Looking out for #1

****

When Eddie gets in trouble, he always seems to drag one of us with him. Well, almost always. This time was different. He only nailed himself. The crazy thing was that everything would have been OK if he hadn't been so selfish with that stupid old baseball. He was just looking out for himself, or, as he likes to say it, he was "looking out for #1."

Now I know you have some things that really mean a lot to you. So do I. You don't want anyone messing with that stuff, right? That's OK. We should take care of our stuff. But Eddie went off the deep end and was just being selfish. About an old baseball!

I've learned a lot from his mistake.

Trying to look out for #2, #3, and #4 first,

Troy

****

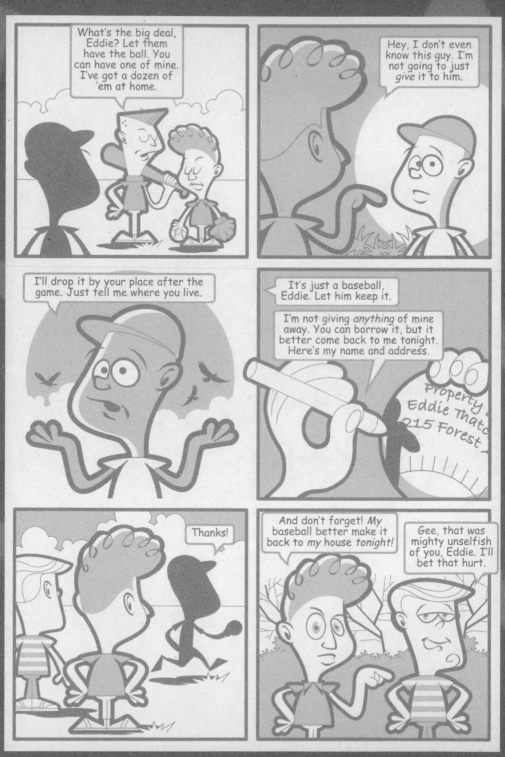

The Foolish Fat Man

We can only imagine how much he weighed, but it probably was somewhere between a piano and a Pontiac. The Bible says that the King of Moab was "very fat." He was also very rich and powerful, and he commanded a strong army. But he was never satisfied. He always wanted *more*. His army attacked and defeated Israel. The king took whatever he wanted from the Israelites and collected taxes from them every year—for eighteen years. He was a very selfish man.

All this time God was using the selfish King of Moab to punish the Israelites because of their *own* selfishness. They had stopped obeying God. They did whatever they felt like doing, so God allowed the King of Moab to rule over Israel. Finally the people of Israel cried out to God for help.

God used a man named Ehud to free the Israelites. When it was time to again pay taxes to the King of Moab, Ehud brought the money to the king. He also brought a little something that the selfish king didn't expect—a sword. The sword was specially made so it could be strapped to Ehud's leg and hidden under his clothes.

In order to be alone with the king, Ehud told the king he had a secret message for him from God. The king sent all his servants out of the room and stood up. Ehud pulled out the sword and thrust it deep into the king's belly. It must have been like stabbing a block of Jell-o. The sword kept going in until it finally stuck out of the king's back. Ehud didn't pull the sword out. He just let go of it and pulled his hand free. The fat closed in around the handle of the sword so that it disappeared! The selfish king fell to the floor, dead. Then Ehud escaped from the king's palace.

Ehud didn't waste any time. He quickly raised an army of Israelites to help him finish the job. They killed about 10,000 of the King of Moab's soldiers and won back the Israelites' freedom. The Israelites had changed. Instead of doing what *they* wanted to do, they were ready to follow God.

Being selfish is never smart. Just look at the Israelites. They paid for their selfish attitude for eighteen years. Better yet, take a lesson from the King of Moab. He always wanted more and more. He was never satisfied. He finally got more than he could stomach. He paid for his selfishness with his life!

Want to read the story of Ehud in the Bible for yourself? Read Judges 3:12–30.

HOW BRAINY ARE YOU?

We can *all* be pretty selfish. The problem is that we don't seem to notice when we are. This quiz may help to open your eyes.

Howie

1.   You and your family are at a restaurant. A plate of buffalo wings is placed on the table. What should you do?
   A.   Grab as many as you can pile on your plate.
   B.   Pick the biggest buffalo wings before somebody else does.
   C.   Hand out the wings, saving the best for yourself.
   D.   Let the others take wings before you do.

2.   You're in the lunchroom at school with a hot extra-cheese pizza in front of you. Your friend forgot his lunch money and looks hungry. You have a couple of bucks in your pocket. What should you do?
   A.   Eat your pizza in front of him, being sure he knows how good it is.
   B.   Pretend you don't notice your friend is hungry.
   C.   Tell him how stupid he is to forget his money.
   D.   Lend him your money so he can get a pizza.

3. **You are being selfish when you**
   A. Won't share a video game with a friend.
   B. Spend the whole $5 on yourself that your mom gave you to share with your sister.
   C. Insist on watching what *you* want on TV even though your brother (or sister) wants to watch something else.
   D. All of the above.

4. **Being selfish is**
   A. Caring about myself more than others.
   B. Caring more about what I want than what others want.
   C. Being greedy.
   D. All of the above.

How did you do?
The right answer in each is the last one.

FAQS

(FREQUENTLY

ASKED QUESTIONS)

I think selfishness is a bigger problem than we realize. It's not just kids who are greedy. Adults are, too. One time when I was over at Eddie's house I heard his mom complaining to a neighbor about how selfish Eddie's dad was. "That's the real reason we got a divorce," she said. "He only thought about himself."

I know I shouldn't have been listening, but what she said got me to thinking. Selfishness isn't something we grow out of when we get older. It's still there, and it can cause a lot of problems. I want to work on being less selfish, so I got some questions together and gave them to that leader at our church. His answers helped me a lot. I think you'll get something out of them, too.—David

1. **Sometimes I don't want to share because I'm afraid my stuff will get wrecked. Does that mean I'm selfish?**

    Not necessarily. It's important to take good care of the things you own. But don't get stingy. Try to be as generous as you can with the things that aren't quite so breakable. When it comes to the more expensive stuff, you may just have to politely say you can't let anyone use it unless you are there.

2. **My sister complains that I insist on doing things my way. What's wrong with that? My way is the best way.**

When you say your way is the best way, that is your "opinion." For example, some people believe that the best way to travel across the country is in an airplane because it's fast. Others would say the best way is to drive or take a train so they can enjoy the scenery. It doesn't mean that any of them are wrong. Or that any of these is the best way. These are all opinions, the ways different people prefer to travel.

You'll be smart if you don't insist on doing things your way all the time. Listen to what others want. Sometimes it doesn't matter whose way you think is best. A really unselfish attitude is to put others first. That sometimes is hard to do, but it's something that will make people appreciate you a lot more. And you know what? You'll grow to be a better person.

3. **If selfishness is so bad, why do so many adults, even Christians, act that way?**

Even though selfishness is wrong, people still act that way. Even Christians. Don't get caught in that trap. When people are selfish, they are disobeying God, no matter what age they are. Check out these verses: Philippians 2:3–4 and 1 Corinthians 10:24. God wants us to put others first.

4. **How do I become less selfish, especially when I don't even realize I am being selfish?**

Don't think you can do this on your own. Ask the Holy Spirit to teach you to be more like Jesus, to show you when you're being selfish and to help you change. You'll be amazed at the difference.

CHAPTER 6

"Eddie and the Homemade stink Bombs"
email from Troy

To: Every guy who could use a little more patience
Subject: Eddie's "bomb" prank

****

Eddie says everybody overreacted. The assistant principal. The police. The bomb squad. Linda Barsky. Everybody.

He was told that his prank was in "poor taste." I don't know about taste, but it sure *smelled* awful. Poor Howie got suckered into it at the last minute.

This stunt took Eddie a long time to collect everything and get things ready. No spur-of-the-moment deal. He sure had patience, but he got a bad payoff.

Real patience is a good thing. But it doesn't come easy for me. When I'm in a rush, or things are going crazy around me, I don't even have enough patience to stop and think about what I'm doing. I get myself in a lot of trouble that way.

I'm asking God to help me be more patient. I also thanked him for helping me *not* listen to Eddie this time. For once I wasn't left holding the bag when his plan backfired!

I can hardly wait to be more patient,

Troy

****

ziklag zig-zag

Kidnapped! Every son, daughter, and wife who lived in Ziklag was gone. When David and his men returned home, they found the town burned to the ground. Everyone was gone. Their families had been kidnapped by an enemy raiding party who were taking them to their own country and would sell them as slaves.

David and his men wept until they were so exhausted they didn't have the strength to cry anymore. Some of the men blamed David. They wanted to kill him.

Here's where David was so amazing. The Bible says that instead of heading right out after the enemy raiding party, David took time to find "strength in the Lord." He took time to pray and ask the Lord what he should do. He didn't want to make a mistake. He must have reminded himself that God was in control. David was patient. Even in a crisis situation he took the time to take his problem to God and ask for his guidance.

David believed God wanted him to take his 600 men and search for the enemy raiding party. The men were so exhausted that at one point 200 of them had to be left behind. David and his remaining band of 400 men pressed on and caught up with the enemy raiders. It was nearly dark, but David and his men attacked anyway. They fought all night and into the next day. The battle went on for about twenty-four hours! They didn't stop for a meal or for rest. David and his men defeated the enemy raiders and rescued all the wives and kids. Not one was lost! David, the leader some of them had wanted to kill earlier, was once again their hero.

We can learn a lot from this amazing story of patience and endurance. We should ask God to help us be more like David. Even when David's life zig-zagged from good to bad, he took the time to pray and spend time with God. When he felt he knew God's direction, he started out and kept going and didn't give up.

This is a great story to read right out of the Bible. Read 1 Samuel, chapter 30.

HOW BRAINY ARE YOU?

I'm asking God to help me out with this whole "patience" thing, 'cause the truth is, I hate to wait! Do you have that problem, too? Take this quiz and find out.

Howie

1.   Is it OK to cut in line if you're in a real hurry or you just can't wait?
  A.   Yes, always.
  B.   Yes, as long as nobody is looking.
  C.   Yes, especially when you have more important things to do and are in a big hurry.
  D.   No.

2.   If you want to use the bathroom, but your sister has been in there with the door locked for a long time, what should you do?
  A.   Bang on the door until she opens it.
  B.   Tell her that her boyfriend is on the phone so she'll come out.
  C.   Threaten to read her email if she isn't out in thirty seconds.
  D.   Ask her nicely to go as fast as she can, then wait.

3.   If you want to skip this question to get to the next chapter, it might show that you are a little _____.
   A.   Irritable
   B.   Overzealous
   C.   Preoccupied
   D.   Impatient

4.   Which of these would show that you're trying to be patient?
   A.   Tapping your fingers while you're waiting for something.
   B.   Saying things like, "C'mon, hurry up!"
   C.   Not bothering to listen to someone else's viewpoint when you're having an argument.
   D.   Holding the door open for someone and letting them go through before you do.

How did you do? Unless you picked the last choice for each of these questions, it looks like *you* hate to wait, too!
—Howie

FAQS

(FREQUENTLY ASKED QUESTIONS)

I'd like to be more patient, but I don't take the time to think about it much. If you're thinking you don't want to take the time to read these questions, you just might have a problem with patience. I got these questions from guys like you. I asked one of our church leaders to take a look at them. He wrote the answers. I know this is going to help me, and bet it'll help you, too.—David

1. **What's wrong with being a little impatient? Doesn't that help get things done?**

    When we're impatient, generally it means we have a problem with pride. Think about it. When I don't want to wait my turn or things aren't happening fast enough for me, my attitude deep down is that I'm more important than the others around me. That attitude of pride is wrong. God hates it, and that's a pretty good reason to ask God to help you to be more patient. One more thought. When we're impatient, we often say something mean or rude or we'll do something inconsiderate in some way. Read Proverbs 14:29 and Ecclesiastes 7:8.

2. **I see my parents get impatient (usually with me) a lot. If they don't seem to care that they're impatient, why should I work on being patient?**

The Bible tells us in Ephesians 6:1–3 to obey our parents, but it doesn't say we're always supposed to act like them. Parents aren't perfect. They can't be. The Bible tells us to be like Jesus. He was totally patient. That's one of the things people must have loved about him. If we want to be more like Jesus, we need to be more patient.

3. **But you don't know my _____ (brother, sister, or whoever). They're so annoying!**

Sometimes God uses annoying people to help teach us patience. If you want to get stronger, you have to do exercises or lift weights so that you really work your muscles. If you don't work the muscles hard enough, you won't get stronger. It's the same with patience. When we are around people or in situations that give our patience a workout, we're in a great position to grow more patient. So if your brother or sister is really annoying, look on the bright side. God may be developing you into a super-patient person!

4. **How can I be more patient?**

Understand that it's hard to make ourselves more patient. The key is to ask God for help. He has given all Christians the Holy Spirit as a helper for many things, and one of them has to do with patience. If we let the Holy Spirit work in our life, we will become more patient. Read Galatians 5:22. Ask the Holy Spirit to help you. When you blow it, ask for forgiveness. Keep going to the Holy Spirit for help. It will take time, so be patient.

CHAPTER 7

"The Homework Assignment"

email from Troy

To: Every guy who's ever told a lie and gotten caught!
Subject: Bamboozling Miss Hollish

****

David got caught in a lie. That's right. *David*. The guy whose head is screwed on a little straighter than the rest of us. It all started in Miss Hollish's class. Guess who was involved. Right again. Eddie. He pressured David into backing up his story, which was a lie. That's how David got nailed.

We all know how easy it can be to lie. We twist the truth a little to get something we want or to get out of trouble.

I'm not talking about big "whopper" lies. It's the little lies that are so easy to say. Some people call them "white lies." Eddie calls them "bamboozling." No matter what you call them, they're lies, and lies are wrong.

I'm learning that sticking with the truth, no matter what, is smarter than telling a lie. And it's the best way to stay out of trouble!

Determined to tell the truth, the whole truth, and nothing but the truth,

Troy

****

THE LIE THAT WOULDN'T DIE

Joseph was an annoying younger brother. He had some pretty odd dreams that he told to his ten brothers, which made them resent him. But the thing that made his brothers extremely jealous was that Joseph was their father's favorite child. Joseph's brothers hated him and even plotted to kill him. But one brother talked them out of it. Instead of killing Joseph, they sold him as a slave. When the caravan bound for Egypt disappeared down the road, Joseph's brothers never expected to see him again.

But they had to tell their father something. So the brothers ripped up Joseph's coat, soaked the pieces in the blood from a goat they killed, and took the bloody coat home to the father, saying they had found it. Their father looked at the coat, recognized it as Joseph's, and decided that Joseph must have been eaten by some wild animal.

At first, it looked like the boys got away with their big lie. Their father was heartbroken, but they got what they wanted—their annoying brother was gone. They didn't realize that nobody gets away with lying forever. Sooner or later the truth comes out. Because God knows.

Years passed. Eventually God blessed Joseph in ways beyond anything his brothers could have imagined. He became a great leader in Egypt. He was second in power to Pharaoh.

When a famine spread throughout the land, the brothers traveled to Egypt to buy food. The man they had to see was their annoying brother, Joseph. But they didn't recognize him. When Joseph finally told them who he was, they were frightened because of what they had done to him. But Joseph told them not to be afraid. He gave them food and invited their families and their father to live in Egypt so they wouldn't ever have to worry about having enough food again.

Can you imagine what happened when the brothers went back home? They had to confess to Dad all the lies they had told. They had to tell him how they had faked Joseph's death and sold him as a slave. For all those years, they hid their lies. But lies never die.

You can read the Bible story of Joseph and his brothers in Genesis 37.

HOW BRAINY ARE YOU?

This whole honesty issue can get a little confusing if you're not careful. Take my quiz and see if it helps clear things up.

Howie

1. **When is it OK to lie?**
   A. If it's a little white lie.
   B. If it will get you out of trouble.
   C. If it will get you something you want.
   D. It's never OK to lie.

2. **Exaggerating or stretching your stories to make them more exciting is a form of lying.**
   A. False
   B. True

3. **What could happen if you're not honest?**
   A. People stop trusting and believing you.
   B. You lose friends.
   C. You get in more trouble.
   D. All of the above.

4. You go to the mini-mart to buy some chips and the clerk gives you an extra $5 in change. What should you do?
    A. Save it for something important.
    B. Keep it because it was the clerk's mistake.
    C. Buy something nice for your mom.
    D. Give it back to the clerk at the mini-mart.

5. You get your math test back and notice the teacher gave you more points than she should have. What should you do?
    A. Show your friends.
    B. Stay quiet so your teacher doesn't find out.
    C. Show your teacher.

Well, did you pick the last answer on all of them? You're right!

FAQS

(FREQUENTLY

ASKED QUESTIONS)

I've picked up some tough questions on honesty from guys like you. I'm glad I didn't have to answer them. I got help from one of the men at my church. Some really good stuff is here!—David

1. **Is it OK to lie so I don't hurt someone's feelings?**
   Lying isn't OK, even when you're only trying to keep someone from being hurt. When you lie to make someone feel better, it's really a form of flattery. The Bible warns against the use of flattery in Proverbs 26:28. The better thing to do is to learn how to be tactful. Learn how to say the truth in a kind way. Sooo, if your mom asks you how you like her new hairstyle, and you think it isn't so great, find a nice way to say it. Maybe something like, "The way you used to have it was my favorite, but ask me in a couple days after I've had a chance to get used to it."

2. **I know regular lies are bad, but what about "little white lies"?**
   A lie is a lie, no matter what color it is. The Bible doesn't allow for "little white lies." In fact, God hates lies. If we want God's blessing on our life, Psalm 34:12—13 reminds us to not lie.

3. **If my parents ask me to tell them the truth about something, but I don't tell them quite everything, that isn't lying, is it?**

    Telling them part of the truth isn't good enough. When you hold back on some of the information or details, you're deliberately trying to give them a false impression. You're giving them a picture that isn't accurate. And that's a lie. There's a story in Acts 5 about a husband and wife who told only part of the truth. Read what happened to them and you'll understand that God considers someone who tells only part of the truth to be a liar.

4. **If I pretend to do something, but I'm really doing something else, is that considered lying?**

    Like if you're pretending to do homework, but you're really playing a computer game, right? That's considered a form of dishonesty. Jesus spoke out against that type of dishonesty. Stay away from that kind of stuff.

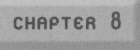

CHAPTER 8

"anger essay"
email from Troy

To: Every guy who has ever lost his temper
Subject: Living up to my nickname, Trigger

****

OK, I'm going to tell you straight up that I lost it. I was ticked, angry, *mad!* Just ask Eddie. He has the broken finger to prove it.

Do you lose your temper? Bad things just seem to happen when we get angry, don't they? Sometime I'll have to tell you how I got the nickname "Trigger." Kids at school think it's because of my quick jump shot in b-ball. But David knows how I really got it. My quick temper earned me the name.

Anyway, I've been trying hard not to "pull the trigger" and shoot off my mouth or do something else stupid when I get mad.

I didn't do so good with the whole anger thing the other day. I'm asking God to help me with that 'cause I sure can't do it on my own.

Learning that it's bad to be mad,

Troy

****

"anger essay"

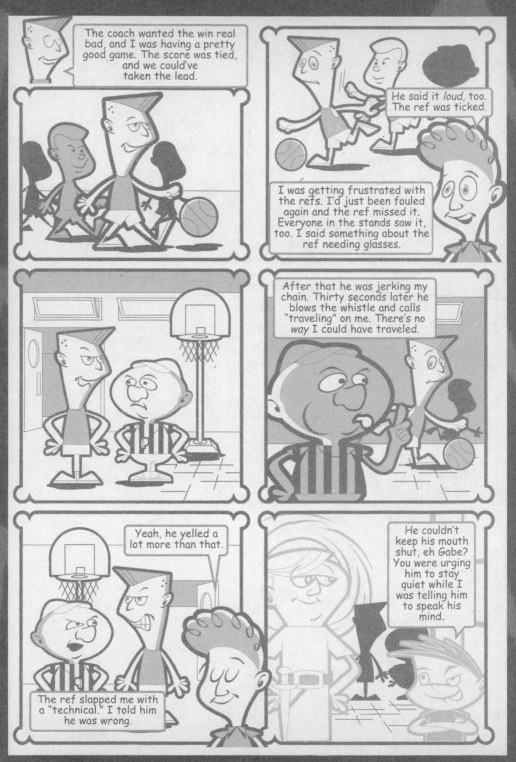

the Hot-Headed King

King Nebuchadnezzar ordered a big dedication ceremony for his new idol, a 90-foot statue. He wanted a band there, and the rule was that as soon as the band started playing, all the people were supposed to bow down and worship the idol.

On the day of the ceremony, the people gathered around the idol and the band began to play. Whooosh! Like a giant wave, the people dropped to their knees and bowed to the ground to worship the king's idol.

But Shadrach, Meshach, and Abednego didn't bow down. They believed in the one true God and wouldn't bow down to the king's idol, even though they worked for the king.

The king was furious! He said they had one more chance to bow down. If they refused, he'd give them a one-way ticket to the furnace. This didn't heat the palace in the winter. The king used the furnace to roast people who made him mad! His message to the guys was simple. Bow down or burn up! The king told them even *God* couldn't rescue them from the flames.

They told the king they didn't *want* a second chance. They knew God *could* rescue them if he wanted to, but they would *not* bow down to an idol.

King Neb controlled thousands of people, but he couldn't control himself. The angry king gave orders to fire up the furnace *seven* times hotter than normal. Shadrach, Meshach, and Abednego were tied up and thrown in the inferno. The heat was so intense that the soldiers who threw them in were killed instantly.

Instead of burning to a crisp, the three guys were unharmed. The king saw them in the furnace with a *fourth* person! God was protecting them. The king described this surprise guest as looking like "a son of the gods."

The king called to Shadrach, Meshach, and Abednego to come out. Everyone watched as the three stepped out of the flames, unharmed. Not a hair on their heads or any part of their clothes was burned. They didn't even smell like smoke. The king and his men pressed in close and inspected the three.

King Neb realized Shadrach, Meshach, and Abednego served the one *true* God. From that point on he treated the three *really* well.

We can learn something from King Neb. When you get a "hot head," you'll find you have a "cold heart," and that's a deadly combination! When you're angry, it's easy to lose control and you can end up hurting yourself, hurting others, or both. Be smart. Ask God to help you keep your temper under control.

Want to read the story of the fiery furnace in the Bible for yourself? Read Daniel 3.

HOW BRAINY ARE YOU?

Somebody once told me, "The person who gets you mad isn't your biggest problem. Your biggest problem when you're angry is the fact that you lose control of yourself."

At first I thought the person who told me that was nuts. Now I'm beginning to understand. If I let myself get really mad, I might do something that will make things worse. A lot worse. I have to be able to control myself. It's a choice. Let's see if you make the right choices on this quiz.

Howie

1.   Your annoying little brother follows you around and embarrasses you in front of others. You're about to leave the house to meet some friends and he wants to come with you. You get mad. What's the best way to handle it?
   A.   Tell him he wouldn't have fun because your friends are all much older.
   B.   Yell at him until he promises not to follow you.
   C.   Sneak out of the house so he doesn't see you go.
   D.   Ask God to help you to calmly talk to your brother about how you feel and to explain why he has to stay home.

2.   When you're mad at someone, it's OK to yell and scream at them, just as long as you don't hit them.
   A.   True
   B.   False

3. What can happen if you don't control your anger?
   A. You might hurt someone.
   B. You might hurt yourself.
   C. You might lose a friend.
   D. All of the above.

4. A friend comes over to your house. As he's heading upstairs to your room he drops your remote control car and it breaks. Instantly you feel yourself get mad. What should you do?
   A. Tell him to go home.
   B. Yell at him and call him clumsy.
   C. Clam up and refuse to talk to him.
   D. Put the broken car away and play with something else.

5. When you're really mad inside, the best way to get rid of your anger is to
   A. Say the alphabet backwards.
   B. Punch a pillow.
   C. Punch someone.
   D. Shoot a prayer to God, asking him to help you get rid of the anger.

How did you do
The right answers were the last ones listed (although some of the wrong answers sounded pretty tempting!).

FAQS

(FREQUENTLY ASKED QUESTIONS)

Anger can flare up in an instant, but the effects of anger can last for weeks, even years. People do some pretty stupid things when they're angry. Troy helped put together some questions on anger. He felt the answers I got from my dad were a big help. See what you think.
—David

1. **If we're not supposed to be angry, what about the time Jesus got so angry that he turned over the tables at the temple?**

   You're thinking that Jesus lost control, right? Maybe you figure that somehow he messed up. Instead of "road rage," maybe Jesus had a "temple tantrum," eh? Let me tell you what really happened.

   Mark 11:11 tells us that Jesus went to the temple and saw "everything." He saw the merchants ripping off the people who came to worship. It must have made him sick. He didn't lose control. It says he left for the night. Now, the Bible says Jesus would get up early each day to pray. I would guess that's exactly what he did. He got up the next morning, prayed, and then walked back to the temple and chased the dishonest merchants out. If Jesus had been "out of control," he'd have chased the men out the first night.

What would a man do if there were robbers in his house? He'd chase them out. That's what Jesus did. The men were robbing innocent people. He observed it, he slept on it overnight, and the next day he took care of it. The Bible says Jesus never sinned. That means he didn't "lose it" at the temple.

2. **Is being angry always wrong?**
   There are times when anger isn't wrong. Jesus' "righteous anger" in the temple is an example. He was angry at men who were robbing innocent people. God can get angry at sin. We might get angry when we hear about an innocent person being arrested or a dishonest judge sentencing that person to a harsh prison term. The key is that this "righteous anger" shouldn't make you lose control and sin as a result. You can't just stay angry, either. You have to bring your anger to the Lord and ask him to help you deal with it. Ephesians 4:26 even tells you when you should do this.

3. **Sometimes I get into an argument and I just want to clobber my _____ (sister, brother, whoever).**
   You need to remember that when you get angry like that, you're not doing God's will. Read James 1:19–20. We like to think that it's the other person who is wrong, but if you're angry about it, you've got a problem too. James 1:20 explains that being angry gets in the way of us living the way God wants us to live. When we get so angry we want to hit somebody, Jesus says it's as bad as murder. That's serious stuff! Read Matthew 5:21–22 and 1 John 3:15. The thing is, that kind of anger is out of con-

trol. We need to be able to control ourselves. You've got to read Proverbs 29:11. It makes it pretty clear that losing self-control when you're angry isn't smart. It's like somebody driving a car when they're drunk. Nothing good can come of that. Pray and ask for help. It works!

4. **I can't help getting mad sometimes. What am I supposed to do?**
    Ask God to help. He gave us the Holy Spirit to live in us, to teach us, and to help us grow to be more like Jesus. But if we don't let the Spirit have control of us, we'll always struggle with anger. We can't beat anger on our own. Just trying harder doesn't work. We need to ask the Holy Spirit to help us. He can change our attitude and take our anger away. It's amazing. He's done it for me many times. Read Galatians 5:22–25.

CHAPTER 9

"Eddie and the Green-eyed Monster"
Email from Troy

To: Every guy who has ever been jealous
Subject: This monster is *real!*

****

When was the last time you got a little jealous of someone? It's easy to say or do something dumb when that happens, isn't it? I don't think I'll ever forget what happened when the green-eyed monster of jealousy got a grip on Eddie. He lost it.

When I was a kid, I was afraid of monsters. I was sure they were real—especially at night. There's no way I was going to go down in the basement by myself! As I got older, I finally figured out that the monsters were only in my imagination and movies.

I'm rethinking that now. Jealousy is one bad monster. I'm praying God will help me fight off the green-eyed monster whenever it comes hunting for me!

Being "green" makes you mean,

Troy

****

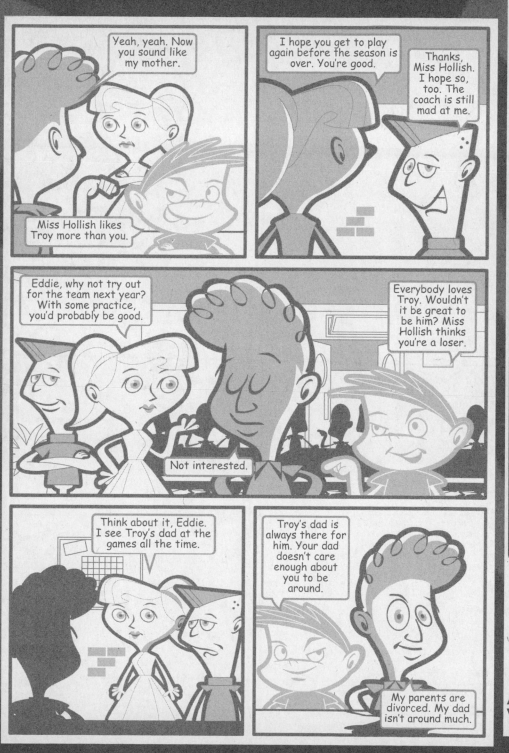

Human shish-kabob

ou've seen shish-kabobs, right? You drive a sharp metal stick through chunks of meat so they can be cooked on a grill. David, the shepherd boy who killed Goliath, almost became a *human* shish-kabob when King Saul got jealous of him.

After killing the giant, David joined King Saul's army. He fought well and became a national hero. People even wrote songs about him. But like a deadly poison, jealousy crept into King Saul's heart and began to destroy him.

One day, while David was playing his harp, the king's jealousy came on stronger than ever. King Saul grabbed his spear and hurled it at David. He wanted to pin David against the wall with the spear! He wanted to turn him into a shish-kabob.

David darted out of the way of the spear, and King Saul tried a second time. Again, David was able to dodge death and escape.

King Saul then sent David on dangerous missions against the Israelites' enemy, the Philistines. The king was secretly hoping David would get killed in battle. But God protected David, so he always came home safe and more popular than ever.

The king got so jealous he could no longer think clearly. King Saul tried again to spear David while he was playing his harp, but he escaped from the palace. That night, King Saul laid a trap for David at his house. Once again, he got away, but this time he decided he would not go back.

David was now on the run, and about 600 men who were loyal to David went with him. The king went berserk! He was crazy with jealousy! Because he thought a priest had helped David escape, King Saul had eighty-five priests and their families killed. King Saul's son Jonathan stuck up for David. King Saul was furious that his son cared about David, and he tried to shish-kabob Jonathan. King Saul wanted to *kill* his own son by running him through with a spear just like he had tried to do to David. Jonathan, too, was able to dodge the spear just in time.

Jealousy can be a real beast. It can *change* you and twist your thinking without you even knowing it. If you want to be smart, don't be like King Saul. He lost his friends, family, reputation, and sanity. Instead of asking God to take the jealousy away, King Saul let jealousy destroy his life.

Want to read the story of David from the Bible yourself? Start in 1 Samuel 17.

HOW BRAINY ARE YOU?

Spell the word *jealousy*—j-e-a-l-o-u-s-y. Now remove the first three letters. What's left is how you feel when the green-eyed monster takes over your life—lousy. I've been thinking a lot about jealousy ever since that little episode in the cafeteria with Eddie. Somehow he twisted everything in his head and got jealous of Troy. And he didn't even know it. Until afterwards. Let's just say I learned that jealousy can be a pretty nasty and sneaky thing. So I put together some questions about jealousy.

Howie

1. **Which one of these could be an example of jealousy?**
    A. Wanting your friend's baseball card.
    B. Being mad because your buddy is better in sports.
    C. Wishing and wishing you had as much money as the rich kid in class.
    D. All of the above.

2. **What should you do when you realize you're jealous of a friend who just won a science fair competition?**
    A. Study harder so next year you can beat him.
    B. Drop him as a friend so you won't have to think about it.
    C. Tell someone he cheated on his project and didn't deserve to win.
    D. Ask God to help you get over your jealous feelings.

3. Jimmy went to Bobby's house. Bobby had just bought an NBA team shirt and matching shorts. Jimmy really wants them. What should he do?

   A. Steal them when Bobby isn't looking.
   B. Beg his parents to buy them for him.
   C. Rip them when Bobby isn't looking so he can't wear them.
   D. Earn the money by mowing lawns or cleaning garages to buy a set himself.

4. Is it OK to be jealous as long as nobody knows you're really jealous?

   A. Yes.
   B. Sometimes.
   C. Depends on the situation.
   D. No.

5. A guy in gym class is so good in sports that he makes you look like a klutz. Sometimes you wish he'd break a leg. The truth is, you're jealous.

   A. False
   B. True

How did you do? If you picked the last choice for each question, you're right!

FAQS

(FREQUENTLY

ASKED QUESTIONS)

I've heard of people doing all kinds of things because they were jealous, but that stunt of Eddie's has to be the weirdest. Jealousy is too dangerous to mess with. These FAQs can help you get control of your jealousy.—David

1. **Just because I'd like to have something a friend has doesn't mean I'm jealous, does it?**

   It's hard to say. There's a fine line between feeling "Hey, I'd like to have one of those" and really becoming jealous. Try to evaluate your feelings. Do you feel a little resentment that your friend has it and you don't? Do you feel he gets all the breaks? Do you feel you deserve it more than he does? Do you feel it's a waste that he got it and that you would have put it to much better use? Do you wish you could somehow take it if you wouldn't get caught? Do you sort of wish it would break so he wouldn't have it either? If you're feeling any of these, you're probably in the danger zone. You're jealous.

2. **OK, OK, so I'm jealous. What can I do about it?**

   Confess it to God in prayer and ask him to change your attitude. Ask him to make you content with the things you have. Be content. Read Hebrews 13:5–6. This is great stuff.

3. **Everybody feels a little jealous once in a while. What's the big deal?**

   Jealousy is sin. Jealousy is what drove Cain to kill Abel in Genesis 4. It's like a monster that can drive people to do bad things. Jealousy is listed right along with idolatry and witch-craft and hatred in Galatians 5:19–22.

4. **What about those verses in the Bible that say God is a "jealous God"?**

   God does get jealous for his people. It isn't a sinful jealousy, because God can't sin. He wants his people to follow him, and him alone, for their own good. When they stray and ignore God, he is jealous in a pure, protective way.

CHAPTER 10

"The palm Reader"
email from Troy

To: Every guy who's had the sick feeling you get after you do something you knew was wrong

Subject: I'm still having nightmares

****

I will not do something I know is wrong.

I will not do something I know is wrong.

Hey, I'd write it a *thousand* times if I thought it would keep me from making a mistake like *that* again. The thing is, I *knew* it was wrong, but I did it anyway. You've been there, done that, right?

I've asked God to forgive me, and I know he did, but I can't seem to forget it. I've scrubbed my hand dozens of times, but I can't wash away that creepy feeling I get when I think about that palm reader. I still get nightmares. The Kid told me that Eddie's been leaving the light on when he goes to sleep at night.

Next time my gut tells me something is wrong, I'm listening! I've learned that it's never right to do wrong.

Asking God to help me do the right thing,

Troy

****

when doing wrong seems right

King Saul had been hunting for David for a long time, trying to kill him. Saul could not get over his jealousy toward the shepherd boy who had killed Goliath and become Israel's national hero. To escape from Saul and his army, David and his band of 600 men traveled all over the country, hiding in caves and anywhere else they could, always on the run.

Finally, Saul and his army were close to catching up with David. They camped on a hill for the night. David and his men were hiding nearby in the desert. Late that night, David and Abishai, one of his trusted soldiers, snuck to the edge of King Saul's camp. The king and his best men were in a deep sleep. Abishai believed God was giving David an opportunity to kill the king.

Abishai's idea made some sense. If King Saul was dead, David would be free. God had promised that David would be king someday. Maybe this was how God had intended for David to become king. Simply kill King Saul and take his place.

But David knew it was wrong. Even though he could have gotten away with it, David wouldn't kill King Saul. He decided it was best to let God deal with King Saul.

Instead, to prove they had really been in the king's camp, David and Abishai crept into the camp and picked up King Saul's water jug and spear that were near the sleeping king's head. They tiptoed out of the camp as silently as they had come in.

When they were a safe distance away, David shouted and woke King Saul and his men. The king was shocked to realize David had been right there in their camp and could have easily killed him, yet he didn't. King Saul felt ashamed. He stopped the hunt for David and went home.

There are times when doing something wrong looks right. Like when we know we can get away with something and nobody will ever know. Maybe we have the perfect opportunity to cheat, lie, or do something else that God wouldn't approve of. Faced with that temptation, we need to remember to do the right thing. That's the smart choice. That's the choice David made. I guess that's just one more reason why God selected him to be king.

Want to read about this in the Bible for yourself? Read 1 Samuel 26.

HOW BRAINY ARE YOU?

Sometimes doing the *wrong* thing is just easier. At least that's the way it seems at the time. Later you feel pretty bad about it. I mess up like that a *lot*, but not quite as often as I used to. So maybe I'm finally getting smarter! Let's see how brainy *you* are when it comes to doing the right thing!

Howie

watch a movie that you know your parents wouldn't want you to see. What should you do?

   A. Watch the movie, but don't tell your parents.
   B. Watch the movie, but try to close your eyes during the bad parts.
   C. Don't worry about it. Just have a good time.
   D. Tell your friends you can't watch the movie. Ask them to watch a movie that would be OK. If they say no, call your parents and have them pick you up.

2.   You're supposed to start your homework as soon as you get home from school. Your mom is still at work and nobody else is at home. What should you do?

   A. Watch TV for a while first, then do your homework.
   B. Make yourself a snack and play a computer game.
   C. Go to a friend's house, but be sure to be back before your mom gets home.
   D. Start your homework.

3.   You're on the Internet and you remember the address of a dirty website a guy at school told you to check out. You know it's wrong to do. Nobody will ever know if you go to the website or not. What should you do?

A.   Try typing in the website just to see if it really exists.

B.   Go to the website, but promise yourself you'll only go there for a few minutes.

C.   Go to the website, but promise yourself you'll never go there again.

D.   Don't go to the website, ever. If it's a temptation, stay off the Internet.

4.   You see your friends at school hide a new kid's backpack. At the end of the day, you see the new kid frantically looking for it. What should you do?

A.   While the kid is busy looking for his backpack, hide his jacket.

B.   Don't do anything. It isn't any of your business.

C.   Don't tell the new kid where his backpack is 'cause your friends might get mad at you if they found out.

D.   Help the new kid out. Tell him where the backpack is.

Some of these were tough, right? It can be so easy to do the wrong thing. If you picked the last choice for each question, you were right!

FAQS

(FREQUENTLY

ASKED QUESTIONS)

It's a lot easier to sleep at night and look my parents in the eyes if I'm not trying to hide something I did wrong.

I'm asking the Holy Spirit to make me more like Jesus, you know, the way he grew in wisdom and favor with God and man. I'm hoping you'll pray for the same thing in your life. And hey, don't forget to read your Bible every day.

Here are some questions we pulled together from guys like you on doing the right thing.—David

1. **How do I know what the right thing is?**
   Read your Bible every day. It helps you learn right from wrong. The Holy Spirit is another huge help. All Christians have the Holy Spirit inside them. Pray for direction when it comes to deciding right and wrong, and the Holy Spirit will let you know which way to go. Finally, get input from your parents or from godly leaders at church. They've lived longer and learned more and generally have a good handle on what's right and what's wrong.

2. **If I do something that is wrong, but nobody gets hurt, is it all that bad?**

    Doing something wrong is sin. When you sin, somebody always gets hurt. You. You just don't realize it at the time. Sin destroys. Stay away from sin whether you can see the hurt or not. Read Proverbs 4:14—15.

3. **Sometimes I want to do the right thing, but I blow it.**

    It can be hard to do the right thing, especially if you try to do it on your own. The more control over your life you give to the Holy Spirit, the more often you'll do the right thing. Rely on the Holy Spirit and his power.

4. **What difference does it make if I do something wrong? God will still forgive me, right?**

    Sure, God will forgive if we ask, but God may have to discipline us if we are that casual about doing the wrong thing. If we are Christians, we should be growing in our love for God. If we love God, why would we deliberately want to disobey him? Read Romans 12:9—21 for some guidelines on how to live.

    Remember that the effects of sin can stay with us even though God has forgiven us. For example, let's say somebody offers you illegal drugs. You know it's wrong, but you take them anyway. While you're high, you climb halfway up a telephone pole and jump off, somehow convinced you can fly. Let's say you knock out all your front teeth, four up, four down. God can forgive you for taking the drugs, but you'll still have the effects of that sin with you for the rest of your life. Every time you look in a

mirror, you'll see a face like a Jack-O-Lantern with its teeth missing. Doing the wrong thing on purpose can be summed up in a single word— stupid.

5. **You don't know what I've done. Nobody does. Can God forgive that?**
Yes. God forgives any and all sin. He's forgiven murderers (the apostle Paul, before he became a Christian, had people imprisoned and approved of them being killed), liars (Peter was a liar), thieves (Zacchaeus stole from people), and every other sinner who has come to him and confessed from their heart. It doesn't matter what you've done. God will forgive you. Read 1 John 1:8–10. Ask him to forgive you, and you can be certain he will. Then ask him to help keep you from falling into that same sin again. See also Jude 24. Finally, ask God to help you do the good things he created you to do in the first place. That's in Ephesians 2:10.

A NOTE TO THE READER

If you're reading this, I guess it means you finished the book. Great job. I hope you grew to like the guys from the "Code 2:52" comics as much I do. I hope you learned from their experiences.

Life really *is* a battle. There really *are* angels, and there really *are* demons. The demons have made it their goal to destroy you. Think about that. They don't want you to grow in wisdom and in favor with God and men, as the verse in Luke 2:52 describes. They don't want you to become more loving toward others; they want you to be more selfish. They don't want you to become more kind; they want you to be more inconsiderate. The demons want you to become more proud and less humble. They want you to be quick to get angry and slow to forgive.

Who are you listening to? When you do or say something, when you make a decision, is it Jesus who influences you to do the right thing? Are you learning to do the right thing from the Bible and the help of the Holy Spirit?

My prayer for you is that you choose to follow Jesus' example. He loves all people with an unselfish heart. He is faithful to God. These are things that you can work on too. Ask God to help you.

Plenty of things that you do or think or say are things you later regret. I hate that feeling, don't you? You'll have a lot fewer regrets if you make the right choices *before* you act or speak. You'll never regret doing or saying things that are kind, humble, unselfish, and forgiving.

Grow to be a man of God. It's the smartest choice you can make. Remember too that what you become is always your choice. Know that I'm praying for you.

Choosing to live for Christ,
Tim

What is  2:52 SOUL GEAR ?

Based on Luke 2:52:
"And Jesus grew in wisdom and stature,
and in favor with God and men (NIV)."

2:52 is designed just for boys 8-12!
This verse is one of the only verses in
the Bible that provides a glimpse of Jesus
as a young boy. Who doesn't wonder what
Jesus was like as a kid?

Become smarter, stronger, deeper,
and cooler as you develop
into a young man of God
with 2:52 Soul Gear™!

Zonderkidz

The 2:52 Soul Gear™ takes a closer look by focusing on the four major areas of development highlighted in Luke 2:52:

"Wisdom" = mental/emotional = **Smarter**

"Stature" = physical = **Stronger**

"Favor with God" = spiritual = **Deeper**

"Favor with men" = social = **Cooler**

2:52 Soul Gear™ Books—

Action, adventure, and mystery that only a boy could appreciate!

Laptop 5: Dangerous Encounters

Written by Christopher P. N. Maselli
Softcover 0-310-70664-5

Laptop 6: Hot Pursuit

Written by Christopher P. N. Maselli
Softcover 0-310-70665-3

Laptop 7: Choke Hold

Written by Christopher P. N. Maselli
Softcover 0-310-70666-1

Laptop 8: Shut Down!

Written by Christopher P. N. Maselli
Softcover 0-310-70667-X

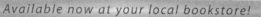

LINTBALL LEO'S not-so- stupid Questions about your Body

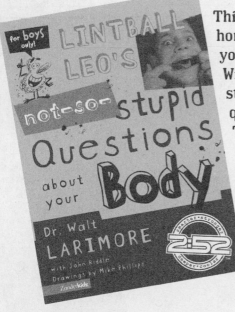

This is the first book for boys that gives honest answers to real questions about your body from a biblical perspective. With information about everything from steroid use to body parts, there's not a question Lintball Leo hasn't heard. These aren't questions some adult made up, but they're real questions asked by real boys just like you. You want to know the truth? Now you can, because <u>Lintball Leo's Not-So-Stupid Questions About Your Body</u> gives you the facts—no holds barred!

Everything a boy should know, but won't ask!

2:52 Soul Gear™ Books–
Action, adventure, and mystery that only a boy could appreciate!

Bible Heroes & Bad Guys

Written by Rick Osborne, Marnie Wooding & Ed Strauss
Softcover 0-310-70322-0

Bible Wars & Weapons

Written by Rick Osborne, Marnie Wooding & Ed Strauss
Softcover 0-310-70323-9

Bible Fortresses, Temples & Tombs

Written by Rick Osborne
Softcover 0-310-70483-9

Weird & Gross Bible Stuff

Written by Rick Osborne
Softcover 0-310-70484-7

Check out other non-fiction books available in the 2:52 Soul Gear™ collection!

The Book of Cool

Written by Tim Wesemann
Softcover 0-310-70696-3

GodQuest

Dare to Live the Adventure
Written by Rick Osborne
Softcover 0-310-70868-0

Available now at your local bookstore!

Coming February 2005 . . .
Another "straight from the pages of the Bible" ACTION & ADVENTURE book!

Big Bad Bible Giants

Written by Ed Strauss

It's all about giants, some in the Bible and some not. Helping you get smarter, stronger, deeper, and cooler, *Big Bad Bible Giants* is full of facts that will fascinate even the most inquisitive reader.

Softcover 0-310-70869-9

Coming February 2005

A new four-book series filled with adventure, mystery, and intrigue as three friends, Dan, Peter, and Shelby, seek to discover the hidden mystery of Eckert House!

2:52 Mysteries of Eckert House: Hidden in Plain Sight (Book 1)

Written by Chris Auer
Softcover 0-310-70870-2

2:52 Mysteries of Eckert House: A Stranger, a Thief, and a Pack of Lies (Book 2)

Written by Chris Auer
Softcover 0-310-70871-0

2:52 Mysteries of Eckert House: The Chinese Puzzle Box (Book 3)

Written by Chris Auer
Softcover 0-310-70872-9

2:52 Mysteries of Eckert House: The Forgotten Room (Book 4)

Written by Chris Auer
Softcover 0-310-70873-7

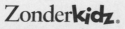

Zonder**kidz**.

We want to hear from you. Please send your comments about this book to us in care of zreview@zondervan.com. Thank you.

Zonder**kidz**®

Grand Rapids, MI 49530
www.zonderkidz.com